The Wednesday Surprise

For Penny Kastanis and her mother Katina Anton,
whose story this is.
—Eve Bunting

For Marjorie Naughton
—Donald Carrick

Clarion Books
a Houghton Mifflin Company imprint
215 Park Avenue South, New York, NY 10003
Text copyright © 1989 by Eve Bunting
Illustrations copyright © 1989 by Donald Carrick

Printed in the USA
Library of Congress Cataloging-in-Publication Data

Bunting, Eve, 1928–
The Wednesday surprise / by Eve Bunting; illustrated by Donald Carrick.
p. cm.
Summary: On Wednesday nights when Grandma stays with Anna everyone
thinks she is teaching Anna to read.
ISBN 0-89919-721-3   *PA ISBN 0-395-54776-8*
[1. Grandmothers—Fiction.   2. Reading—Fiction.]   I. Carrick,
Donald, ill.   II. Title.
PZ7.B91527Wf   1989

[E]—dc19   88-12117
                                                   AC
HOR   20 19 18 17 16

The Wednesday Surprise

by Eve Bunting

illustrated by Donald Carrick

Clarion Books

NEW YORK

I like surprises. But the one Grandma and I are planning for Dad's birthday is the best surprise of all.

We work on it Wednesday nights. On Wednesdays Mom has to stay late at the office and my brother, Sam, goes to basketball practice at the Y. That's when Grandma rides the bus across town to stay with me.

I watch for her from the window and I blow on the glass to make breath pictures while I wait. When I see her I call: "Sam! She's here!" and he says it's okay to run down, down the long stairs and wait by the door.

"Grandma!" I call.

"Anna!" She's hurrying, her big, cloth bag bumping against her legs.

We meet and hug. She tells me how much I've grown since last week and I tell her how much she's grown, too, which is our joke. Between us we carry her lumpy bag upstairs.

I show Grandma my breath picture, if it's still there. Mostly she knows what it is. Mostly she's the only one who does.

On Wednesday nights we have hot dogs.

"Have you heard from your dad?" Grandma asks Sam.

"He'll be back Saturday, same as always," Sam says. "In time for his birthday."

"His birthday?" Grandma raises her eyebrows as if she'd forgotten all about that. Grandma is some actress!

When Sam goes she and I do the dishes. Then we get down to business.

I sit beside her on the couch and she takes the first picture book from the bag. We read the story together, out loud, and when we finish one book we start a second.

We read for an hour, get some ice cream, then read some more.

Grandma gives me another hug. "Only seven years old and smart as paint already!"

I'm pleased. "They're all going to be so surprised on Saturday," I say.

When Sam comes home we play card games, and when Mom comes she plays, too.

"You'll be here for the birthday dinner?" Mom asks as Grandma is getting ready to leave.

"Oh yes, the birthday," Grandma says vaguely, as if she'd forgotten again. As if we hadn't been working on our special surprise for weeks and weeks. Grandma is tricky.

"I'll be here," she says.

Sam walks Grandma to the bus stop. As they're going down the stairs I hear him say: "What have you got in this bag, Grandma? Bricks?"

That makes me smile.

Dad comes home Saturday morning, and we rush at him with our *Happy Birthdays*. He has brought Sam a basketball magazine and me a pebble, smooth and speckled as an egg, for my rock collection.

"I found it in the desert, close to the truck stop," he says. "It was half covered with sand."

I hold it, imagining I can still feel the desert sun hot inside it. How long did it lie there? What kind of rock is it?

Dad has stopped to pick wildflowers for Mom. They're wilting and she runs to put them in water. Then Dad has to go to bed because he has been driving his big truck all through the night.

While Dad sleeps, Sam and I hang red and blue streamers in the living room. We help Mom frost the cake. We've made Dad's favorite dinner, pot roast, and our gifts are wrapped and ready.

I watch for Grandma and help carry the bag upstairs. Wow! Sam should feel how heavy it is now! Grandma has brought a ton of books. We hide the bag behind the couch. I am sick from being nervous.

Grandma usually has seconds but tonight she doesn't. I don't either. I can tell Mom is worried about the pot roast but Grandma tells her it's very good.

"Are you feeling well, Mama?" Dad asks Grandma. "How are your knees?"

"Fine. Fine. The knees are fine."

Dad blows out the birthday candles and we give him his gifts. Then Grandma shoots a glance in my direction and I go for the big bag and drag it across to the table. I settle it on the floor between us.

"Another present?" Dad asks.

"It's a special surprise for your birthday, Dad, from Grandma and me."

My heart's beating awfully fast as I unzip
the bag and give the first book to Grandma. It's
called *Popcorn*. I squeeze Grandma's hand and
she stands and begins to read.

Mom and Dad and Sam are all astonished.

Dad jumps up and says: "What's this?" but
Mom shushes him and pulls him back down.

Grandma has the floor. She finishes
Popcorn, which takes quite a while, gives the
book back to me and beams all over her face.

"My goodness!" Mom is beaming too.
"When did this wonderful thing happen? When
did you learn to read?"

"Anna taught me," Grandma says.

"On Wednesday nights," I add. "And she
took the books home, and practiced."

"You were always telling me to go to classes,
classes, classes," Grandma says to Dad. She
looks at Mom. "You must learn to read, you say.
So? I come to Anna."

I giggle because I'm so excited.

Grandma reads and acts out *The Easter Pig*. And *The Velveteen Rabbit*.

"It's much smarter if you learn to read when you're young," she tells Sam sternly. "The chance may pass along with the years."

Sam looks hurt. "But I *can* read, Grandma."

"Nevertheless." She takes out another book.
"Are you going to read everything in that
bag, Mama?" Dad asks her. He's grinning, but
his eyes are brimming over with tears and he
and Mom are holding hands across the table.

"Maybe I will read everything in the world
now that I've started," Grandma says in a
stuck-up way. "I've got time." She winks at me.

"So, Anna? What do you think? Was it a good surprise?"
I run to her and she puts her cheek against mine.
"The best ever," I say.